My Naughty Little Sister

and

FATHER CHRISTMAS

Dorothy Edwards' 'MY NAUGHTY LITTLE SISTER' is an unforgettable character, one who generations of children have warmed to, and it is a great privilege to be given an opportunity to create her visual image.

This Christmas story depicts her at her most typical; not so very naughty really, so much as extremely determined to get what she wants. From the first time I read Dorothy's stories about her I had a very strong image of what she looked like; and bringing her to life on the page has been one of the most enjoyable interpretive work I have ever done.

Shirley Hughes

My Naughty Little Sister and Father Christmas

DOROTHY EDWARDS

Shirley Hughes

EGMONT

When I was a little girl, my naughty little sister was pleased
when Christmas began to draw near, because she liked
all the excitement of the plum-puddings and the crackers, and
all the Christmassy-looking shops, but she didn't like to think
about Father Christmas at all — she said he was a *horrid old man*!

There – I knew you would be shocked at that. But she did.
And she said she wouldn't put up her stocking for him.

My mother told my naughty little sister what a good old man Father Christmas was, and how he brought the toys along on Christmas Eve, but my naughty little sister said, "I don't care. And I don't want that horrid old man coming to our house."

Well, that was bad enough, but the really dreadful thing happened later on . . .

One day, my schoolteacher said that Father Christmas would be coming to the school to bring presents for all the children, and that he would have toys for all our brothers and sisters as well, if they cared to come along for them. She said that there would be a real Christmas tree with candles on it too.

When I told my little sister
about the Christmas tree,
she said, "Oh, nice!"

And when I told her
about the toys she said,
"Very, very nice!"

But when I told her about
Father Christmas, she said,
"Don't want him, horrid old man."

But my naughty little sister did want to go, very much, so she said, "I will go, and when Father Christmas comes in, I will close my eyes."

So, we all went to the Christmas tree together, my mother, and I, and my naughty little sister.

When we got to the school, my naughty little sister was so pleased to see the holly and all the pretty paperchains, robin-redbreasts, and little lanterns we school children had made she smiled and smiled.

Then, when all the children sang, my little sister smiled even more, and she sang too. She sang, "Away in a manger" and when she didn't know the words of some of the singing, she "la-la'd".

After all the singing, the teachers put out the lights, and took away
a big screen from the corner of the room . . . and there was the
Christmas-tree, all lit up with candles and shining with silvery stuff,
and little shiny coloured balls. There were lots of toys on the tree,
and all the children cheered and clapped.

Then the teachers put the lights on again, and the candles, so that we could all go and look at the tree. My little sister went too. She looked at the tree, and she looked at the toys, and she saw a specially nice doll with a blue dress on, and she said, "For me".

My mother said, "You must wait and see what you are given."

Then the teachers called out, "Back to your seats, everyone, we have a visitor coming". So all the children went back to their seats, and sat still and waited and listened.

And, as we waited and listened, we heard a tinkle-tinkle bell noise, and then the schoolroom door opened, and in walked . . .

. . . Father Christmas.

My naughty little sister had forgotten all about him, so she hadn't time to close her eyes before he walked in. However, when she saw him, my little sister stopped smiling.

Father Christmas was very nice. He said he hoped we were having a good time, and we all said, "Yes," except my naughty little sister – she didn't say a thing.

Then he said, "Now, one at a time, children; and I will give each one of you a toy."

So, first of all each schoolchild went up for a toy, and my naughty little sister still didn't shut her eyes because she wanted to see who was going to have the specially nice doll in the blue dress.

But none of the schoolchildren had it.

Then Father Christmas began to call the little brothers and sisters up for presents and then he let them choose their own toys off the tree.

When my naughty little sister saw this, she was so worried about the specially nice doll, that she thought that she would just go up and get it.

So, my naughty little sister got up without being asked to, and she went right out to the front where Father Christmas was standing, and she said, "That doll, please," and pointed to the doll she wanted.

Father Christmas laughed and took the specially nice doll off the tree. He handed it to my naughty little sister and said, "Well now, I hear you don't like me very much, but won't you just shake hands?" and my naughty little sister said, "No". But she took the doll all the same.

Father Christmas put out his nice old hand for her to shake and be friends, and do you know what she did?

She bit his hand! She really and truly did. Can you think of anything more dreadful?

She bit Father Christmas's hand, and then she turned and
ran out of the room with the doll held very tightly in her arms.

Father Christmas was very nice. He said it wasn't a hard bite, only a frightened one, and he made all the children sing songs together.

When my naughty little sister was brought back by my mother, she said she was very sorry, and Father Christmas said, "That's all right, old lady," and because he was so smiley and nice to her, my funny little sister went right up to him, and gave him a big hug, which pleased him very much.

And so my naughty little sister hung her stocking up after all, and that kind man remembered to fill it for her.

And my little sister kept the specially nice doll until she was
quite grown-up. She called it Rosy-Primrose, and although
she was sometimes bad-tempered with it, she really loved
it very much indeed.

To all naughty little sisters everywhere,
and their long suffering older siblings.
S.H.

EGMONT

We bring stories to life

My Naughty Little Sister and Father Christmas originally published as
'The Naughtiest Story of All' in the title My Naughty Little Sister
written by Dorothy Edwards, illustrated by Shirley Hughes, and first published in
Great Britain in 1968 by Methuen Children's Books Ltd.
This edition published in Great Britain 2019 by Egmont UK Limited,
The Yellow Building, 1 Nicholas Road, London W11 4AN.
www.egmont.co.uk